Contemplating Creation

Anuradha Gajaraj-Lopez

Copyright 2021© Anuradha Gajaraj-Lopez

United States Library of Congress

Control No: TX0008975146 / 2021-05-27

ISBN: 9798742262022

Sri Agastya Gnana Peetam Publications

Dedicated to

My Paramaguru

Sri Sri Swami Yukteswar Giri

The Epitome of Knowledge

The physical world operates under one fundamental law of Maya, the principle of relativity and duality...To remove the veil of Maya is to uncover the secret of creation.

Paramahansa Yogananda

(Pg. 266-267 Autobiography of a Yogi 1997)

MOMENTS IN ETERNITY

He dipped his quill into the fountain of love
And wrote this beautiful poetry we call life
What are we but,
Sparks of his great divine light?

Like a dew quivering gently
On a freshly opened petal
Dancing for a moment
In joyous abandonment,
In this vibrant tapestry we call life!

Here for a moment, gone the very next
Our very existence, but
A moment in eternity!

❀

Table of Contents

Foreword

When I met Anuradha Gajaraj-Lopez at a Tai Chi class, I was struck by her effortless flow, as she went through the slow motions of the Tai Chi form. It seemed apparent to me that she was not just going through the motions, there was something deeper. This was confirmed during our very first interaction. I felt she had a deep inner knowledge of her 'self'. These years knowing her, has given me an insight into her spiritual thought process.

Her open-mindedness, adaptability, and vision have given me a deeper understanding of different spiritual paths, including being introduced to the fascinating world of yogis, saints, and sages.

As an organizational psychologist, I study human behavior in organizations and workplaces scientifically. I always see the bigger picture of how behavior in our distinctive individual cultures has a larger global effect. This idea is a recurring theme in her book. As she says in the chapter 'Knowledge – Existing and Yet to Come',

"Since every created thing was interconnected in the tapestry of God's thought that we call creation, each one of them had an influence on everything else."

She draws the reader through an intriguing journey from the moment of creation, to what was, is and what could be. She never loses sight of the core theme of ourselves as spiritual beings in her narration throughout the book.

This book is for anyone who has asked themselves the question "why were we created?". Tapping into her understanding of comparative religion, Anuradha brings forth her wealth of knowledge on the subject in the book that she jokingly calls, "a spiritual fantasy-fiction".

Yet, her writing is more than fiction. It helps one understand that the essence behind all religions whether it is Christianity, Islam, Hinduism, or any other is the same. That they are all ultimately based on the same truths as she contemplates on 'why creation'.

Affirming that we each are on our individual journey through our own spiritual process, the book is a wholesome and positive look into the world as it can be. All we have to do is open our hearts.

Enjoy your path and this terrific journey!

Lillian J Fillpot, PsyD.

Preface

Countless people have wondered from time immemorial on the eternal questions that continue to remain a mystery. What is creation? Who are we? Why were we created? Why this creation?

Great masters have come to the earth from time to time to give us some answers. Yet, the reason for creation has remained a mystery. Different religions have attempted to answer these questions. We have the story of Genesis in the Bible; we have the Bhagavad Gita giving its version. Native cultures have their own stories of creation. All of them talk about how creation took place and what our goals are.

Yet, the very idea of 'why creation' has never been answered. All we know from our scriptures is that it is beyond human comprehension.

Belief is that those that know cannot express through the limited tool of human language. Another argument is that once you 'know', the 'you', no longer exists.

Yet we know that whatever this 'understanding' is, it is not beyond the reach of any man. If at all, we do not 'know', it is because of our lack of trying to 'know'. Or perhaps, our fruitless search to know the 'unknowable' through human concepts like logic, rational thought process, and science.

Science has progressed to an extent where we continue to discover the seemingly endless vastness of the universe. We are discovering that there are particles of matter that are smaller than the smallest matter we have discovered so far.

Scientists are finally beginning to acknowledge that vast amount of energy is contained in seemingly small particles.

We are beginning to understand that there are realms beyond our physical senses that science is only discovering, albeit very slowly.

What was known to our saints and yogis, that the human body is not just made up of physical matter, is finally becoming a more accepted idea.

Kirlian photography has been used to record auras around human beings. Science has rejected it because mankind has become so mired in the idea of the material world. Yet, clairvoyants through the centuries have seen things that no ordinary physical eyes can see.

At the other end of the spectrum are so many things that we can see that we are yet unable to understand. The mysteries of why there are huge monoliths laid in exact patterns is not yet known. What power motivated this exercise which needed superhuman strength or at the best advanced technology?

Remnants of works that seem to defy our idea of primitive man's capabilities abound like the stone heads of the Easter Island leading us to question Darwin's theory of evolution.

Unable to get an answer to these questions, I thought, how about just letting my imagination run and see where we arrive? This book is that result of that flight of fancy.

❀

BEFORE TIME

Creation

Long before the earth as we know was created, there existed a great void. It was a pure effervescent and boundless joy-filled void[1]. It was the supreme power manifested as the unmanifested. The process of creation was about to begin. Love, knowledge, and expression was its very nature.

From that void emanated a continuous roaring sound inaudible to the created world. This was the primordial sound of creation. From this sound appeared seven distinct beings. These were the first of the created. Ever present, they would remain through the different cycles of creation. They would be the guides for all that was to come.

They were given the power to retain complete knowledge of their divine origin. They were to remain on the earth plane through the eternally ongoing cycles of creation and dissolution. With the power to assume any form needed, they could take the form of saints, celestial beings, angels, or whatever a created being called for in true devotion.

And so, the seven lights oversaw the world as it was being created. First came the distinction between light and dark. Then came the distinction between space and matter. Thus, duality came into existence, and would continue to play the part of separating the manifest from the unmanifest.

Universes were created, galaxies, stars, planets came into being. Many were the planes where creation took different hues. Life was breathed into some of the planets. One such was the earth. Here, before man as we known him could make his advent, the foundation

------

[1] Primordial sound: Called the Aum by the Hindus, Amen by the Christians, and Amin by Muslims.

for the created earth would be laid.

Meanwhile, the act of creation of universes continued, forever expanding with billions of universes, endlessly, quiet unfathomable to the modern human mind.

Till today, no man has been able to explain the cause of this great phenomenon. Not in a clear rational way anyway.

Perhaps, expression being its very nature, creation was never meant to be a deliberate act. The primordial force was simply 'being' itself. It was doing what it was meant to do: express. And in that expression was indescribable joy. Joy that only those that realize their own 'self' as the creator would eventually understand.

For the want of a better word, we shall call this primordial force – God. God of all religions, God of all universes. God of everything that was, is and will be. One God. Formless and omnipresent.

Concept of Time

It was a period when, 'time' as we know it, did not exist. Everything took place in the 'now'. The definite linear movement of time that we have come to widely accept was not recognized as the truth then. Since everything was but a thought of God - just a concept, 'time' could not be measured.

The sun and the moon visibly coexisted. Night and day were one and the same. All that was occurring or was going to occur already existed in the 'thought' of God.

Every event was meant to be available for eternity. Any being that transcended its limitations to understand its true nature as part of the creator would be privy to this knowledge. Such a being could easily tap into events of any period. That was the cosmic plan.

To the current logical mind, a parabola could be used as an example to explain this idea. A parabola is a curve where any point on a directrix is equi-distant from the focus point. If we consider man as the focus point, then linear time is the directrix. All points of time translated from the directrix into the parabolic curve can then be concentrated at the single focus point. Then, man, as the focus point in our analogy, experiences the past, present, and future simultaneously.

Hence, everything that was, is and will be existed at the same time. The idea was that man simply had to tune into that true concept of 'time'. The goal was for man to have that self-awareness, of oneself as a continuous, ever-present fraction of creation. Yet this plan never came to fruition.

That is because, we, shall we call ourselves the "Material Man," see only a fraction of the 'now'. We refuse to consider the concept that everything that existed from the beginning and all that is yet to come is ever present. We fail to understand that the past, the present and the future are all part of the infinite now.

This knowledge was true then and will remain true until the end of creation. But we have lost sight of this truth.

The idea of sound came next.

Power of Sound

Sound being the first emanation in creation, was instilled with a potency that lay latent until used with two important features: pronunciation and intent.

Sound was given power to change the vibrations of the created world. Since sound was the first emanation, music which is based on sound, was to be the foremost of the arts.

Rightly composed music would have the power to light lamps[2] or start rain[3]. And with the right words, pronunciation, and intent, it would evoke devotion and lift the consciousness higher.

And so, the scriptures of the world in the future, would record that it was sound that emanated first when creation began. The singular primordial sound of creation would later be known as Aum to the Hindus, Amin to the Muslims and Amen to the Christians.

Yet it was written that Material Man would lose sight of the potency of sound. He would not know that it is the intent behind the sound that gave power to sound. Loud and jarring compositions would take the place of all that was divine in music. Such would be the power of illusion!

More importantly, few would also know that more important and valuable than sound was silence. In silence, and in interiorization alone would be revealed the mysteries of life and of creation.

Just as the foundation of everything was being laid, so were the

----

[2] Deepaka Raaga: A tune of the classical Hindustani style of music in India. Legend has it that the famous musician Tansen, in the court of Akbar, was able to light lamps with the power of this tune.

[3] Megha Malhar: Also, a tune of the classical Hindustani style of music in India. This tune is said to produce rain in the area when played.

languages of the world yet to come already being recorded. Only the order in which they were 'developed' by man would determine the hierarchy of the oldest language. The story of the Tower of Babel[4] would contain this truth.

That all languages are interconnected would not be understood. At the best, future man would think that the languages emerged from two of the oldest languages according to him: Sanskrit and Latin. Yet, the basis of all languages was the primordial sound of Aum.

Yet long before Sanskrit or Latin were discovered or spoken, another older language would already be in use – Tamil[5]. This language would be given by one of the Gods directly to one of the seven lights. It would remain a language known to be in uninterrupted use from the Era of Gods to the end of this cycle of creation.

The only clue that this was older than Sanskrit or Latin would lie in the fact that it would use poetry in the oldest of its works. In literature, poetry is the highest form of expression since it contains great meaning in few words. Poetry that required great command over language would already be well in use in this the oldest of languages.

One of the first languages where the power of sound was implicit was Sanskrit, known as the 'language of the Gods'. The Vedas[6] composed in Sanskrit and believed to be given divinely to mankind, would stress on the value of pronunciation and the power of sound.

A recitation of scripture following these basic rules of pronunciation and intent would be called 'mantras[7]. So were composed thousands

---

[4] Tower of Babel: Genesis 11:1-9 an origin myth to explain why people speak different languages.
[5] Tamil: A language spoken in southern India. Known to be in use as early as 1st century BC in the form of poetry. It is considered the oldest surviving classical languages of the world.
[6] Vedas: Ancient Indian scriptures believed to be directly revealed to sages. They discuss philosophy, meditation, rituals
[7] Mantra: A word or sound repeated with concentration.

of potent verses in the Vedas that carried much power.

Recited with devotion and intent, and with the correct pronunciation, these mantras had the ability to change the vibrations and create beneficial changes to the physical, emotional, and mental states of those listening and those reciting.

Mankind would see devotional hymns in different languages that would evoke spiritual awakening. Hymns and prayers would always stir the hearts of those listening. It would be the underlying memory of the primordial call that would impregnate these divine renditions. It did not matter what religion future man would associate it with.

Bells in the temples, churches, synagogues, the call of the muezzin[8] from the mosques, and other places of worship would be a reminder of the cosmic nature of sound – the sound of God.

Future world would see one unifying factor in the world where worship was concerned. Everyone would invariably be called to deeper prayer by the power of sound and divinely inspired music.

After the creation of time and sound, came the idea of creating beings to populate the different layers of the worlds.

---

[8] Muezzin: A person who calls Muslims to prayer from the minaret of a mosque.

The Era of Gods

Planets in different universes were peopled with beings – all different from the other. Billions of years would pass before any of these created beings would start wondering if there existed other life forms in the universe.

Layers and layers of realms were created in each universe. These were filled with Gods, angels, goblins, and other creatures too fantastic to even imagine. Among these were also life forms on different planets that would be considered 'alien' in the future based on the mere fact that they were differently made.

On earth, preparation was on for the masses to come. Before the dinosaurs roamed the earth, the geography as well as the composition of the earth was quite different.

Our earth-world consisted of several layers of existence. Each layer was just a thought away from the other. This was when the veils between the different levels of existence was not yet drawn. So, the astral, the physical and causal levels[9] of existence were all free flowing.

Many living and nonliving things were created. Gods and angels were created. Of these, the most important was Man. He was in effect the essence of the creator himself. In him, the creator had hidden all

---

[9] Physical, astral, and causal levels: There layers of existence based on the level of vibrations. The highest level is a layer said to vibrate at highest frequency and hence the highest heavenly region; astral is between physical and causal. Also vibrating at higher frequency and hence not visible to physical realm, but visible to clairvoyants. Physical level is the gross level of densely vibrating matter that we know as our physical world. Theosophical belief is that there are four other planes above the causal plane bringing the total number of planes to seven.

the powers that he himself had. So man would be known as the microcosm of the macrocosm[10].

Gods and the humans of the Era of Gods lived in harmony. These humans were like the present humans, but with superhuman faculties. These would later be described in the legends of the City of Atlantis. Tall, golden hued or blue beings that were blessed with super intelligence and strength. They still retained the knowledge of their connection to the creator as they walked the earth plane. For ease of reference, we shall call them Superior Man.

Gods of the Greek, Indian, Chinese, and other cultures walked the earth and played out their various dramas that one day would be considered legends.

In Greece, the gods were ruled by Zeus, the king of Gods; in Rome Jupiter, in India Indra, in the modern day Denmark, it was Odin. And so there were Gods representing everything from attributes like chastity, wisdom, passion as well as elements like earth, rain, and fire.

They could appear and disappear, transform, or morph and had powers untold and wrought much magic in the world.

It was a time when the animistic concept was real and accepted as a matter of fact. Elements like water could change form into humans or Gods. The interplay between the created beings was very fluid. Hence would come the stories of Gods like Zeus – the God of skies and hence rain, in the Greek pantheon or of Varuna, the God of rain in the Indian legends.

In the Indian legends, rivers would assume feminine forms, thus giving rise to the legends of River Ganga descending to the earth[11].

---

[10] Macrocosm: Cosmos. It is believed that the structural composition of the cosmos is also inherent in man. Hence man is the microcosm of the macrocosm.
[11] River Ganga: Also known as Ganges is considered a holy river in India. Legend has it that she was a celestial being brought down to earth as a life giving river to revive thousands who had perished owing to a curse.

Together, Superior Man and the Gods started using the idea of language, developed architecture, travel and all those other aspects that constitute existence and continuation of life for humanity.

Superior Man would repeatedly show that he was more powerful than Gods. For Gods had limitations set by the creator. They were created only to undertake certain functions. Superior Man, on his part could transcend all limitations, for, he was made in the image of God-the creator.

So, would come the stories of the power of Samson, Hercules, Quetzalcoatl, Horus, Laozi, Thor, and Beowulf.

In India, the drinking of the ocean by Sage Agastya[12] as described in one of the legends, would be perceived as fantastical during the time of Material Man. The sacred Shangri la[13] would not be veiled from the non - discerning man, yet. It would be open for any who sought its waters of knowledge.

It was a land of immense beauty. Flowers shimmered in magical colors and celestial swans swam in the cobalt blue lakes. There were the great sages imparting knowledge to all those who came seeking it.

The seven great lights were spreading around the world taking different forms when necessary, as various prophets and saints, bringing divine knowledge to the earth world.

All these divinely shared knowledge would metamorphosize into stories, folklore, and legends in the future. These would carry the divine knowledge in seemingly innocuous stories that were considered at the best fantastic and entertaining. This was deliberate, to allow for

---

[12] Sage Agastya: One of the sages of ancient India who is credited with retaining his mortal body even today. He features in historical texts of India from the times of the Vedas to the present. According to one legend, he was called upon to drink the waters of an ocean to reveal demons who were hiding beneath it. He is said to have used his yogic powers to drink the entire ocean.
[13] Shangri La: A mythical city in the Kunlun valley

easy transmission of great truths through the ages. In the future, few would care to discern the great knowledge and metaphysical truths behind these.

While the Greek, Roman, Mayan, Aztec and Oriental Gods were playing out their acts in other parts of the world, India was witnessing the interplay of cosmic characters.

The foremost was Adi Para Shakti. In her the Hindu religion equated the concept of the primordial energy. She was that which existed before creation and that which would enable dissolution. She was the endless one. The one with and without form. Adi Para Shakti was also the embodiment of other Goddesses' of the Hindu pantheon.

Kali, by far the most ferociously depicted form, was known as the destroyer. She symbolized the concept of time. It is said that she represents the dark void that was before creation. Among the male Gods, the foremost was Brahma the creator, Vishnu the preserver and Shiva the destroyer. There were countless other Gods playing out what is called their 'lilas[14]' or earthly dramas during this time.

However, Hinduism would always hold the central concept that God, the creator is formless. It was based on the idea that everything manifest or unmanifest emanated from the creator. This idea would enable the Hindus to pray to anything – an idol, a stone, a tree, or a place, and to know that every prayer would ultimately reach that one God - the creator.

Ancient Hindus also understood that in personifying different attributes of Gods in human forms, prayer to the formless creator would be that much easier for man once the veil of illusion was drawn over mankind. Islam would always hold the formless presence of God true to heart.

Yet, for Material Man, anything that could not be proven would not

––––––––––––––––––––––––

[14] Lila's: A Hindu concept of divine play.

make any sense. He would be so heavily dependent on his five limited physical senses that he would forget his divine knowledge and heritage. Henceforth, all these interplays would become legends.

❁

Significance of The Number Seven

The Era of Gods also hid a potent clue to the mysteries of the universe in the number seven. Future man would discover that he had seven main energy centers in his body. Spiritual leaders and sacred texts would incorporate the idea of seven all over the world. The creators would leave the number seven hidden in plain sight in all of creation for the created to see.

The number seven would find mention in all religions. It would find mentions in legends and in philosophy. It would find mention in the energy centers or chakras as they are called. It would find mention in the planes of existence, in attributes, and in geographical areas and concepts.

In philosophy or metaphysics, seven would be associated with the seven main internal chakras or energy centers. These seven energy centers would be known as Mulaadhara, Svadishtana, Manipura, Anahata, Vishuda, Ajna and Sahasrara.

The chakras would correspond to the seven areas along the spine. The base of the spine, sacral, solar plexus, heart, throat, middle of the forehead and crown of the head. Thus, when a person in the stage of the Material Man, attempted the long process of returning to his creator, the spiritual energy at the base of the spine, known as kundalini[15] would ascend from the base of the spine to the crown of the head.

Interestingly, the planes of existence would also be understood as being on seven levels. Philosophy would call it the physical, astral, mental, buddhic, spiritual, divine, logoic, and monadic planes[16].

---

[15] Kundalini: Spiritual energy located at the base of the spine.
[16] Planes of existence: According to theosophy, the physical is the plane of gross

The discerning man attempting to return to his original form, as part of the creator, would evolve from the dense materialistic vibrations of the physical world to the finer vibrations of the divine plane. This practice in the future would involve yoga and meditation.

Christianity would hold the number seven sacred as the days of creation. Seven would repeat in the Bible, mainly in the books of Genesis and the Revelation. Their metaphysical meaning would be hidden to many, or worse, misinterpreted. Seven were the demons driven out of Mary Magdalene[17].

The feast of Passover would be celebrated for seven days by the Jewish people. Seven would also make up the days of the week and the seven colors of the rainbow.

Seven would find mention in Islam as the number of heavens and hells. In the Hindu religion seven would associate with the Saptarishis[18]. China would have the seven sages of the bamboo groove and Greece its own seven sages.

The seven headed snake on the crown of a human form would be seen in both Mexico and India geographically far apart in the modern world.

Despite the recurrence of the same ideas and same number, Material Man would overlook the unity in the teachings of all religions.

He would not give thought to the significance of the seven seas, the

---

matter, the astral is a finer counterpart of the physical plane where the we go after death; the mental plane according to Anne Besant is the plane of consciousness working as thought; the buddhic plane is known as the plane of pure consciousness according to C. W. Leadbetter; spiritual plane according to George Winslow Plummer is where spiritual beings of more advanced nature exist; divine plane is where all souls are born and descend to lower planes; the logoic plane is the highest plane of oneness and beyond that is monadic plane is where the over soul exists.

[17] Mary Magdalene: A woman disciple of Jesus Christ who followed him and was witness to both his crucifixion and resurrection.

[18] Saptarishis: Seven great sages of ancient India and regarded as the patriarchs of the Vedas.

seven hills, or the seven continents. Thus, would the truth be hidden from the deluded man. So, what else happened during the Era of Gods?

Knowledge - Existing and Yet to Come

The period of the Era of Gods would provide the foundation for all the knowledge that would exist in the created world. It would be the knowledge that would be one day 'discovered' by Material Man.

It would be the knowledge that would lead to 'enlightenment'. It was the knowledge that would lead people to believe that they had 'invented' something.

All that was to come - history, literature, discoveries, inventions, and even the life and events and every thought of every human to come would be recorded in the Era of the Gods. This would be present in what many call the 'Akashic records'[19] today. Much of this knowledge would in time be 'lost', just to be rediscovered.

These truths would be hidden in legends, myths, and architecture and structures around the created world. The Material Man would wonder what these meant. The Stonehenge would hold its mystery, as would the heads in the Easter Island. In the East would be found giant footprints on rocks in Thailand, India, and Sri Lanka.

Future man would marvel at the prophecies of 'seers' like Nostradamus. In India, Sage Agastya[20] would take the lead in recording the life of every man to take birth on the earth plane.

Since every created thing was interconnected in the tapestry of God's thought that we call creation, each one of them had an influence on everything else.

Hence, the position of planets and stars would influence the

---

[19] Akashic records: Is a compendium of universal events, thoughts, words, emotions, and intent that ever occurred in the past, present or future of entities and life forms.
[20] Sage Agastya: Credited with creating Agastya Nadi Jothidam, a system of foretelling the life and fate of individuals of the world.

destinies of mankind; the waxing and waning of the moon would influence the vibration of the earth. At the considerably basic level, this would be seen as the tides in the oceans. Stones and gems would exert vibrations that could amplify energy and healing.

The knowledge of astrology, astronomy, medicine, and mathematics was already codified in the cosmic vibrations. Future man, while focusing his mind on that primal 'radio', would connect to these vibrations and take credit for 'new discoveries'.

That would explain how something written as fiction in one period of time would become reality in another. Future man would have a Jules Verne writing about submarines in his book 'Twenty Thousand Leagues Under the Sea', long before the submarine was invented. Leonardo da Vinci would write in detail about flying, long before airplanes were invented.

This would also explain how different humans, seemingly thousands of miles apart geographically could arrive at the same deductions to any problem.

India contributed greatly to the fields of science, architecture, medicine, astrology, mathematics and even astronomy. Here great texts of medicine that included not only cataloguing of diseases that would plague mankind, but also the various methods of healing them, were being written. The methods of surgery including plastic surgery[21] and types of instruments to be used were being documented. Air travel[22] and space travel was being written about. So was the concept of zero[23] and astronomy.

---

[21] Sushruta Samhita: An extensive text found in the Vedic literature not only contains copious information on diseases and their cures, but also contain drawings of surgical instruments and even mentions plastic surgery.
[22] Maharishi Bharadwaj is credited with inventing a flying machine that is claimed to have been able to fly on earth but also between planets. Mention is extensively made of flying chariots as well as vimana as the flying machine was called in the epic Ramayana.
[23] Brahmagupta is credited with recording the concept of zero around 400 BC and

The Aztecs and Mayans would equally contribute to the knowledge of mathematics including the concept of zero. Many future civilizations would claim the sole credit for developing certain concepts including zero. Yet, no one civilization or man could really lay claim to this knowledge. For, all knowledge, known and unknown, emerged from the creator.

Future man would look at this incredulously and pay no greater attention. Some would try to find the truth using logic and rationale. Always the truth would remain elusive until the right time.

Future man would one day understand that he only had to tune in to receive these truths. In the beginning these would come as scientific discoveries and creative work of future scientists and artists.

Future architects would draw from the vast treasure of architectural knowledge and secrets, albeit limitedly. For, they would try to create with reason and instruments instead of using deep concentration and thinking. One pointed focus would be the key to the discoveries made by the scientists, and inspiration of the artists of the future.

Of all men, the men leading mankind's way to the ancient wells of knowledge would be yogis[24] – the ones who embarked on the internal journey of realization. Yogis would make conscious efforts to know themselves, thus understanding the great mysteries behind creation.

In Christianity it would be great saints like Saint Francis of Assisi, Saint Theresa of Avila; in Hinduism masters like Paramahansa Yogananda, Ramakrishna Paramahansa; Viveknanda; and Ramana Maharishi.

In China, Lao Tzu would start the most profound schools of thought called Taoism. Based on the concept of living in harmony with the rhythms of the universe, this simple yet profound path, would attempt to get to the very simplicity of creation – by focus on just 'being'. It

---

Bhaskaracharya in century 1114 AD with the concept of infinity in mathematics.
[24] Yogis: Practitioners of yoga or meditation.

would promote unconditional acceptance and urge men to flow with the rhythm of the universe.

Yet, the secrets of the universe would not be hidden from many who discovered it within themselves. They would unobtrusively return to their original 'self' – as part of the creator. These men or women would never feature in stories or legends. However, their mark would be felt among the few who would be destined to know them.

Inexplicable Architecture

Future generations would marvel at the massive structures around the world, that contain so many secrets. They would marvel at the mystery behind the Gjantija[25] complex in Malta, on the carvings on Mayan temples that resembled space travel or, at the colossal work on the pyramids.

In India, great technology would be used to create temple structures with gigantic stone pillars carved with precise geometric designs[26]. An entire temple complex would be carved top down into a mountain[27]. Archeologists of the future would estimate the construction to take more than a hundred years. Yet discover that according to recorded history it was completed at a fraction of that time. The temple would stand at an impressive height of 107 feet untouched by the passing fancies of life.

Elsewhere in India, stone pillars[28] depicting various musical instruments would emit the sounds of those musical instruments when tapped. These musical pillars of the Vittala temple complex in Hampi would remain for the modern man to discover and wonder. Scientists

---

[25] Gjanjtija: Two temples surrounded by a massive wall with some megaliths exceeding five meters in length.

[26] Ancient Indian architecture throughout the country features innumerable temples and shrines that defy logic regarding the precision of stone carving of the ancient day sculptors. Of particular interest are the famous *Belur-Halebid* temples in the southern state of Karnataka. In the north is the Sun temple of Konark. To mention them all would take up volumes.

[27] The *Kailasa* temple are the largest rock cut temples in the state of Maharashtra. It is still unclear how this temple which appears to be carved in from the top of the mountain was made.

[28] Musical pillars of *Hampi*: There are 56 stone pillars in the *Vijaya Vittala* temple complex in *Hampi*, in Karnataka. They emit the music corresponding to the instrument carved on the stone pillar when struck.

from around the world would attempt to find out the science behind the stone emitting musical notes and fail. For these were not built as structures of mere brick and stone but by using the untold creative power that superior man instilled in the carvings he created.

The megaliths and ancient architecture would be scattered all over the world. Megaliths[29] and structures that are humanly impossible to assemble or construct would confound the modern man.

The largest manmade block of stone in Baalbek, Lebanon would be one such structure. Measuring 64 feet by 19.3 feet by 18 feet these blocks of stone would be estimated to weigh 1650 tons, yet how these were moved and assembled modern man would never discover.

In Laos, thousands of giant urns carved in stone would be scattered around the Plain of Jars, located in the Xianghkhoang plateau in modern earth. Legends would talk about a race of giants and theories would abound for the reason these urns were hewn. Modern man would speculate that they were burial sites and even breweries.

None of these structures would be lost to the modern world. Modern scientists would try fruitlessly to discern the secret behind these structures. Tourists would flock to these places in the 20th century, marveling at these inexplicable architecture. They would hardly understand the significance of such ancient structures that defied logical explanations. These would come to light at the predestined time when future man would understand how to tap all knowledge in the world, by tuning the frequency of his mind to cosmic knowledge.

❦

---

[29] Megaliths: Are huge prehistoric stones that were used to construct a monument or a structure. Europe alone has over 35,000.

Travel and Communication

It was also a time when communication and travel would not need physical faculties. Everything would be mental. All that would change with the advent of 'Material Man'.

Travel between the several planes, including the physical and astral, would be matter of fact. However, in the future, some individuals would catch a glimpse of the astral plane while still in the body and claim that they had indeed been to heaven.

They would not understand that anything was possible in the astral plane. If man believed that it was heaven, his thoughts would create all the beings including the deity based on his belief. If such a person returned to earth without going through the stage of death of the physical body, he would indeed claim he had been to heaven and seen God. He would not understand that 'God realization' was not that easy.

In the west, the great city of Atlantis would thrive, and in what is the South America today, the precursors of the Mayan and Aztec civilizations would receive sacred knowledge that they would immortalize in their architecture.

Future fiction of materializing in different locations as shown in the famous Star War series was happening. Teletransportation was an accepted fact. Future man would see strange sculptures that resembled space craft, see drawings and artistic renderings of strange beings that are unknown to him and wonder at them.

He would be at a loss to explain how ancient man could move huge megaliths from place to place or carve sculptures and decorative pillars with such precision.

Indian mythology and the Vedas would refer to flying machines. Mayan and Aztec architecture would show sculptures that resembled space pods. Future man would marvel at the images that depicted space travel. For, travel between the different worlds was actually taking place then.

Standing testimony to this would be large geoglyphs[30] found in different locations in the world. While seeming inconsequential when seen from land, they would show up as deliberate designs when viewed from above. How did these geoglyphs happen before the modern flying machines were invented? There were proving that the concept of flight was not a modern invention by their mere presence.

So would future man find huge spirals ranging from those carved in the Nazca desert in Peru covering about 19 square meters, to the largest discovery in the Thar desert in India covering 100,000 square meters. How could it happen, if not for advanced technology and an existing system of air travel?

---

[30] Geoglyphs: Large design or motif on ground that would only appear in their entirety when viewed from above or a distance, covering vast areas of land with durable elements.

Spiritual Centers

This was also the time when centers of spiritual power were being created all over the world in specific spots for the ages to come. Among them, in the Middle East it was the location of the Kaaba[31] shrine, in the East it was at Mount Kailash in the Himalayas and at Tiruvannamalai[32] in Southern India. Jerusalem was preparing for the coming of Christ.

Other centers included the area where the great pyramid would be erected in Egypt, Machu Pichu in Peru, and Sedona in the United States.

Some of these natural wonders would be unsurmountable by man. One example would be Mount Kailash[33]. Considered the cosmic axis or center of the world, Mount Kailash would retain its mysticism through time. Modern man would conquer Mount Everest that towers 2000 meters over Mount Kailash, but never Mount Kailash.

Many would fear climbing the Mount Kailash owing to religious beliefs, others would try, but never succeed. Tales would abound about how people were prevented from climbing this mountain owing to mystical reasons. Some would believe that anyone approaching too close to the mountain would experience confusion rendering it impossible to proceed further. Others would claim that they faced sudden onset of severe weather conditions that forced them to turn

---

[31] Kaaba: Is a building at the center of Islam's most important mosque in Saudi Arabia.
[32] Tiruvannamalai: A hill in southern India in the state of Tamilnadu, now famous for the ashram of the spiritual giant Ramana Maharishi. It is said the very hill represents Lord Shiva who assumed the form of a pillar of fire here.
[33] Mount Kailash: Located in the Transhimalaya region of the Ngari Prefecture, in the Tibetan autonomous region, China.

back.

Meanwhile, the precursors of the Greek, Egyptian and other civilizations were experiencing the events that would one day become legends as well.

Science and technology that was being disseminated divinely would in the future become new discoveries or mysteries that would not be solved until much later. The city of Atlantis[34] was still not 'lost', but a living breathing bustling city filled with highly intelligent and spiritual people.

These centers would contain immense power and retain that power until the end of this cycle of creation. Future men would flock to these places, but not all would be able to draw from their power. Little would future man understand, just merely visiting these places would not suffice. He would have to visit these places with complete devotion and receive the energy present in these centers.

So also would the places touched by the great ones carry positive vibrations through eternity. Places of worship would be built in these hallowed grounds. Everyone coming to such a place would gain at least a little blessing because of the giving nature of realized masters. They would gain these blessings even if unaware of the power and sanctity of such places.

All this was ready to help man regain his lost heritage as part of the creator. Man was meant to enjoy life as the created and return once satisfied to his original form – a microcosm of the macrocosm. Creation had been meant to be a joyful experience of expression.

❧

---

[34] City of Atlantis: A fictional island in Plato's works.

41

Evil and Good

This was also a time when there was no concept of good and evil. That which was the result of creation – the negative side of the positive, would be later considered evil.

How this negative devised a way to keep creation going and keep man shrouded in the current world, we will explore shortly. For the moment, let us keep in mind that the negative we refer to here was not 'bad' or 'evil'. It was simply the manifestation of duality that is required to maintain creation.

In the age of the Material Man this concept of there being neither good nor evil, would be profoundly expounded by the Sufi's[35]. Since the very basis of all existence is God there would be nothing that is evil that could come from such a source. They would neither desire heaven nor fear hell.

Some other religions would talk about evil as everything that is contradictory to good. Evil would be identified as that which harms another than the self. But always, there would be solutions or corrections that could be made to right any wrong.

In the highest of realization of future man, duality would no longer remain. Hence there would be no identification with either good or bad. They would simply understand that everything is meant to be.

❁

---

[35] Sufi's: Islamic mystics that emphasizes introspection and spiritual closeness with God.

Quest for Youth and Eternal Life

The period of the Gods and Superior Man would also explain one of the obsessions of future man. Behind the endless quest for the elixir of life and the preserving of endless youth, would be the unremembered knowledge of the Superior Man that had existed in the Era of Gods.

Future man would never be satisfied with his term of life. He would always want more. He would always want to live longer. So future man would investigate into the field of alchemy or try to invent potions to find a way of prolonging life.

Even the idea of nourishing creams for the physical body, or the obsession with maintaining weight - all these would stem from the subconscious desire for eternal youth and an immortal existence that man once possessed during the Era of Gods.

In the age of the Material Man, humans would unsuccessfully attempt to prolong life of even in people afflicted with diseases that caused much pain. They would not understand that the will to live is God given. Once the will to 'live' was lost, nothing would hold life back in the human body. Many would attempt to simply prolong the life of the physical body of another– no matter how broken.

In this pursuit of prolonging the existence of the physical body, Material Man would lose sight of the most important thing. That of correcting one's mind, thought, actions and behavior to progress towards liberation from the confines of creation.

And so humanity would sink from its lofty heights of the Superior Man to the darkness of the Material Man. Here would occur all that is negative. Murder, rape, incest, theft, lies, greed. Even innocent babies and animals would not be spared, as Material Man would fall to the depths of ignorance.

Drugs, alcohol, and misuse of God given faculties would take hold of the mind of the Material Man shielding him from the truth of what he really was: a beautiful and pure replica of the creator himself.

Thousands would remain totally oblivious to the very purpose of life. Caught in the web of their own habits, they would helplessly go through life from one addiction to the next. And return to do it all over again.

Not all the warning of scriptures would awaken them from the nightmare they would make of their own lives. Lust, greed, gluttony, theft, wrath, sloth these would obscure the beauty of the soul resting in each man.

So how is it that humanity fell to these depths?

DRAWING OF THE VEIL

Misstep

We had a beautiful world that was prepared for us during the Era of Gods. The foundation was laid. Knowledge was available to be drawn upon when needed. And we had the seven lights always ready to guide us. Yet, we lost sight of our divine heritage. We are now mired in the world that to us is very real. A veil has been drawn between us and all that was our rightful heritage.

What was it that caused this great veil of illusion to be drawn over mankind?

The negative forces that came into being when the supreme being started his cycle of creation was what we call Satan or Maya. This power knew that if Superior Man retained his knowledge of his divine origin, it would not be long before creation would end.

Every created being would return effortlessly to the creator and that would draw the curtain on the very existence of Satan. So, Satan asked the creator to give the created man the gift of 'choice'. The choice to regain his divine heritage or remain in the created world.

With that one decision, everything changed. A huge rumbling sound began as the vibrations of the different levels of existence started separating from each other. This, the physical earth experienced as a great shakeup. All the knowledge was hidden. The free interplay between worlds and plane of existence ended.

The great civilizations where God and Superior Man co-existed, disappeared from earth. Some structures were destroyed, some submerged. Some left remnants of their existence here and there. These the Material Man would see but not comprehend.

A veil was drawn between the different layers of existence. Beings on the physical earth could no longer see the other layers of existence that they had once been privy to. Only that which vibrated in the grosser frequency of the created world would remain. Gods and Superior Man would no longer be visible to the current world. The story of Adam and Eve would be the metaphor for man losing the knowledge of his divine heritage.

Material Man, who could have walked with Gods had lost his divinity. The freedom of choice that Satan had asked the creator to bestow to man, had become his undoing. For, with free will, man is now making many wrong choices. Like Adam and Eve, in breaking one of God's most important laws – of complete allegiance to God's laws, we have made our journey back to the creator a most arduous task.

It was also so simple. All we needed to do was always do the right thing. The laws were all laid out for us beginning with the Ten Commandments, to the Vedas, and the scriptures of all the major religions in the world.

Choice used wrongly was man's first downfall. And with that came the concept of 'doubt' of everything that man could not understand. Doubt which was diametrically opposite to faith has made the world man's prison. Man is imprisoned in his physical body, in his limited thinking and perception, unless he makes the conscious effort to understand his divine heritage.

Satan or Maya constantly keeps Material Man in the limiting consciousness of the created world. This constant struggle between the real and unreal has created untold drama in this created world. Having lost our divine heritage, we have committed major mistakes. We have forgotten that there is a connection between all that is created. The planets, the stars, the elements, the earth, and man are all interconnected, but we no longer see it.

This consistent wrongdoing has resulted in creating imbalance in the created world. So, what was not meant to happen has been unleashed: plague, disease, floods, earthquakes. The list of natural disasters as we know today is endless.

Yet, in the story of Pandora's box we can see the one thing that can save mankind yet. Hope. As the predestined period comes to pass, we will slowly begin to understand and recover our lost knowledge.

We will still be able regain our lost heritage. But it will be a long time before that happens.

The journey has begun. Scientists like Albert Einstein have discovered quantum physics and have finally declared, "where science ends spirituality begins". A few men have received direct knowledge from the great lights. We have had avatars like Christ, Mohammed, Buddha, and Agastya to mention a few who have come to help us on our way.

Among us, the struggling mankind, only few have complete mastery over the two key factors: breath and stillness to reach great spiritual heights. Yet, all over the world, an increasingly large portion of mankind is finally beginning to explore within: through yoga or meditation.

Some among the thousands striving for spiritual evolution have received knowledge and are beginning to share this. They are sometimes looked at with doubt by the rest of us. We are unable to comprehend that each one of us can go higher on the rungs of spiritual evolution. So those that have not attained the status of God realization are seen with incredulity, or even considered frauds at the minimum.

The Here and Now

So what happened once the veil was drawn? After the great turbulence shook the earth, the geography of earth as we currently know, started forming. Continents were connected, and earth looked vastly different. Some of the original mountains like the Alps and the Himalayas remained. However, some inland seas had turned into deserts.

It was here that life as we know it, formed from a single cell to the time of the dinosaurs. The progress from the cell to the other living organisms, slowly expanding into higher life forms took thousands of years.

Then came man and the progress from animal faculties to the more sophisticated human appearance. When reason was once again breathed into this miniature component of the macrocosm – Material Man, as we are known, our eventual return to the creator began.

As Christ said, man is made in the image of God. We have seven energy centers (Chakras[36]) in our body, corresponding to the seven original created beings. Passage through these chakras by conscious interiorization will bring us back from our limited human existence to the immanent super conscious all-encompassing existence as we finally perceive ourselves as part of the creator.

Great lights like Christ have come to remind us of our origin. But, having drawn the veil of illusion, we are still unable to tear down the veil easily. Humanity has expanded its activities from merely sustaining the physical body as a hunter-gatherer, to advancing in science and technology.

------

[36] Chakras: Seven main energy centers in the subtle human body.

So, consumed are we with life on the physical earth, we have no idea of what lies beyond our five senses. We know only what we can see, hear, touch, taste, and smell.

Save a chosen few who have made the effort to walk on the spiritual path and find God, we, the rest are lost in the world of materialism.

The hidden lurking memory of divinity has spurred some men on the path of higher knowledge. They too have used the key instruments of focus and stillness. However among them, some have chosen the wrong path. With the veil of illusion still drawn tightly, the message they draw from the Akashic records are garbled.

So have come people like Hitler who have committed heinous acts, all in the quest of the divinity that mankind once had. Except, in Hitler's case, his garbled reception of knowledge meant that it turned into a destructive force aimed at certain groups of humanity.

We, humans clothed in different hues, have forgotten that it was the same life energy that created all of us. Wars are fought, and atrocities committed in the name of superior religion or race.

Meanwhile, some have been able to depict some of the higher truths in works of art. Some artists who are closer to the idea of the creative power, owing to the very nature of their work, are trying to understand the concept of the inner workings of the subtle man which is closer to his divinity.

So, they have created statues and icons of spiritual lights like Buddha with his distinct hair. Little does man know that he is looking at physical representation of the thousand flowered Sahasrara[37] (chakra) found in the subtle body of man, on the top of the crown of Buddha's head.

Halos are drawn around saints and Gods. Many are not aware that

---

[37] Sahasrara: The energy center on the top of the head known as the thousand petal lotus which is reached at the end of one's internal journey through meditation.

the auric field when viewed with clairvoyant sight reveals highly evolved humans with this golden light around their head. Yet, that is what these halo's represent.

We have forgotten the significance of the benediction of the palm. We have forgotten simple things like the palms and the feet of man are areas from which cosmic energy can be dispersed in benevolence.

From that forgotten idea has come the practice of bowing at the feet of great ones and elders that originated in India. Millions perform the actions and yet, do not know its significance. That energy is passing from the feet to the one who is bowing at the feet.

Only a few today understand this concept. They are the ones studying systems of healing like pranic healing[38]. It is a science that relies on the use of cosmic energy to heal diseased body parts. Man does not remember that we do not have to rely on gross matter for sustenance or healing. In short, man has forgotten the immense power that lies within him.

We are still in the exploratory stages as we rediscover more and more of the hidden knowledge.

---

[38] Pranic healing: Revived by Master *Choa Kok Sui*, used prana (life energy) to direct healing energy to diseased parts of the body.

Our Lost Heritage

Yet, during the cycle of creation, apart from those that make the effort to realize their divine origin, few will ever know the truth behind their existence. Much of the multitude of humanity of the future will never discover this great truth, that they are indeed the essence of the creator himself!

Thousands of years have passed since mankind evolved from microorganisms to the early homo sapiens, and eventually into the current fully developed human form. The final phase of this cycle of creation began when man finally evolved into a thinking, intelligent being.

How ironic, that the process of dissolution of this cycle of creation would begin with the first steps of the intelligent man. But such is the law of the universe.

Those who realize their divinity while on the earth plane will find liberation from this eternal cycle of creation and dissolution. However, multitudes will never grasp the truth. At the end of this cycle of creation, they will become a senseless mass in the dissolution process, only to return and go through the whole process again.

This knowledge or journey to self or god realization will be long and arduous. It will involve interiorization; and of meditation balanced with right living. For, the great truth is beyond the ken of the ordinary man's waking existence. It is beyond logic and rationale.

Yet, many a man will make that special internal journey. Many will reach the final stage of oneness with the creator. The saints, the angels, the prophets walking the earth from time to time, will help this progress. Of these, the seven lights will be the main guides.

Men experiencing astral travel in their dreams, create their own little dramas. Such is the latent power the creator had bestowed upon us.

53

It is in the sub-conscious mind during sleep that Material Man will experience what it is to be a creator.

Dreams will occur predominantly around the strongest thoughts of that period in that individual. Yet, some will remember lives lived before in flashing scenes, and wake up with the haunting feeling of having been somewhere else before. In waking many will simply dismiss these visions as 'dreams'.

Past life regression sessions when correctly experienced, will show many a Material Man what he has been before in one of his many lives. He will witness scenes that are necessary to help him deal with issues that modern science has not been able to help him with. He will wake up from such sessions, totally confused. Knowing that the person in the past life was also him and the one in the current physical body was also him. And he will realize that God has mercifully veiled the memory of his previous lives so he can start afresh and progress in this one.

The futile attempts to trace ancestry based on biological lineage would one day lose its luster. Once man realizes that he is not reborn in the same biological families through his different incarnations on earth, he will realize that he is not connected to just one family lineage, but entire humanity.

Having all this knowledge, having all this guidance, yet we fail to see that within the little body of flesh and blood, is always present the essence of Go the creator. We have not yet discovered the power of the seven spiritual centers within us. Man does not know the significance of why there are these seven energy fields within himself.

❦

The Plan to Keep Creation Going

With the freedom of choice, Satan or Maya now has a plan to keep creation going; ignorance has taken root. Sins have been made alluring to keep us blinded from our divine heritage. Greed, lust, gluttony, anger, pride, jealousy, and temptation are playing havoc on mankind.

The strongest allure is the ego. That tiny 'I' consciousness, forever binds most of the created, unless we can break free from the veils of illusion.

Among those who try to realize their divine heritage, many are sidetracked. They gain inherent powers in their internal journey. They hear sounds that are not audible to the physical realm and can glimpse the different planes of existence; see Gods and other divine beings; have the power to bring into existence whatever they desire. Instead of ignoring these in search of that final goal - of God realization, they are stepping aside, basking in the glory of praises and adoration of other humans.

The few who ignore this, have, and will attain their goal. They will finally escape this physical plane. But millions will remain steeped in ignorance, never ever realizing what a great heritage they carry.

These souls return time and again during the cycle of creation until the final dissolution of this cycle of creation. Satan's plan seems to be working at least during this cycle of creation.

In the larger scheme of things, creation and dissolution will begin all over again after each cycle had ended. And the souls that did not achieve their divine heritage, will come forth in the next cycle of creation, as the play of creation and dissolution continues endlessly.

Meanwhile, we who hold much trust in science will not accept anything as truth until it can be proven by science or by our limited physical faculties. Yet, to confound us or maybe to remind us, there are extant much of what remains from the Era of Gods.

Through all this, the seven great lights are continuing their work tirelessly to help and aid Material Man regain his lost heritage. Or at the least, bear the results of our own mistakes.

The Gods and Superior Man may have gone behind the veil. However, the seven lights have remained on this earth plane as Material Man began his descent into ignorance. They will be here after thousands of years have passed, when Material Man will slowly ascend again to understand what had been hitherto hidden beyond his physical senses. Their work is not done until the end of the cycle of creation.

Is the future hopeless? No. We may not have the ability to do anything about our past except to learn from what transpired. But the future is yet to come for the world as we know it. We must continue to explore the possibilities of the story of continuation of the created world, and the eventual dissolution in this cycle.

❀

Back to Good and Evil

We had touched upon good and evil in the very first section of the book. There were negative forces during the Era of Gods like demons who did not conform to the purpose of creation. Though we see instances of demons eating other created things during that time, there was an absence of cruel intent. These demons were more like animals during the Era of Gods. They were simply acting on instinct.

We need not have arrived at this sorry state. We have made our journey back to the creator that much more difficult by exercising the use of our free will wrongly.

Material Man has gone over and beyond survival and right living. With free choice, we have overextended ourselves in the realm of creative power. Albeit negatively. Instead of focusing on survival and self-preservation, we have added the negative traits of lust, anger, greed, pride, delusion, and jealousy to our lives. Hinduism calls it the six negative traits that prevents man from knowing his true divine self.

In Christianity, there are seven: pride, greed, lust, envy, gluttony, wrath, and sloth. Islam lists them as belief in many gods, witchcraft, the killing of the soul, using wealth procured unjustly, using the wealth of an orphan, to escape from the battles and slandering chaste women.

Whatever we call these, these can be termed misuse of our free will. Instead of using the gifts of senses given by our Father, the creator, we are now misusing them indiscriminately.

Of all the sins, the two most important ones that are direct anthesis to our creator's plan is murder and suicide. For, man who has the infinite seed of creative force in him, has one power that has not been given to him. It is the power to actually breathe life into a new being. Life, which is the sole reason we exist on this earth, is a special gift from our creator, that cannot be taken lightly.

Science may claim that life forms when the sperm enters the ovum, but who gave the power to the sperm? Who sustains all that exists? Science has not been able to answer that vital question.

Whether it is killing someone else or killing ourselves, we simply do not have that right to take a life. Instead of allowing the plan of creation to unfold in its infinity beauty, we have transgressed, and how!

One need only to read with horror the cruelty that man has shown on his fellow humans. We have done it consistently through the dark ages to now. Whether it was burning witches at the stake or torturing someone who did not confirm to prominent belief systems, we have not spared even our saviors.

How far have we fallen that we crucified the one who walked this earth in the human form to show us that we were created in God's image?

We continue to do this repeatedly. The combination of lust and anger has made man worse than any created creature. Take for example the rape of a woman in India by six men. It was not just the rape, but the cruelty that followed that sends chills through our spine. Use of an iron rod to thrust into the woman and pull out the entrails even as she was alive - can anything transcend this horror? Grown men using infants, babies, children in lust for two minutes of pleasure? Where are we headed? How hard is it to keep the great purpose of God in our hearts as we see the horrors of the modern world?

Yet, we cannot lose sight of the fact that Man has indeed been made in the image of the creator. And that seed that is latent within us can be nurtured. Each one of us can make a difference to the world. All we need to do is change ourselves. One character trait at a time, one moment at a time. Hope is not lost. God's plan of creation cannot go awry, no matter how far we fall below the standards of right living. And we will always have the seven lights guiding us. Ever guiding us, patiently. We simply must ask for guidance.

A FUTURE IN OUR HANDS

Looking Ahead

Having attempted to understand our past and while experiencing our present, the thought of what is next crosses the mind.

We have seen the Gods and Superior Man build the foundation for life on earth. We have seen Material Man destroy it slowly but surely. The earth is getting hotter, we are yet to find another habitable planet. Our scientists have not yet discovered if other life forms exist in the universe. If and when they do, we still do not know whether we can coexist with them in peace. We, who cannot even exist with each other in peace, how can we change ourselves when confronted with something alien to us?

Material Man in his eagerness to discover and invent, has brought mayhem and strife into this world. Nuclear energy that could be used for great good has been used to devastate entire cities.

What is it that is yet to come? Are we going to see more of the devastation and nature's fury? Is there going to be a third world war? Will the world as we know it continue?

The questions are many. It does not look like we have much to look forward to. We know that despite all that is happening, millions continue to be oblivious to the higher truths. The transition from the Material Man to the ascending stage of the Thinking Man is but beginning.

At the time of writing this book, the world is in a state of shock because of one tiny invisible virus. Normal life as we knew it, has come to a grinding halt. We are having to change the way we live, as this tiny virus invisible to our eyes, is spreading havoc in our lives.

We are no longer meeting our larger families or friends. We are no longer congregating in our communities to celebrate or mourn. Man is essentially beginning to see his world shrink to the few he lives with.

Our faces are now covered as we carefully wash and rewash our hands and sanitize everything we touch. We do not even hug one another. Solitude is being forced on many who are not used to it.

Still worse, businesses are closing. People are losing their livelihood. The changing world is affecting all our lives. The very technology that made the world a smaller place, has ensured that this virus has spread covering every geographical location.

What may have taken years to spread, has taken only a matter of few months. Our air travel has ensured that. Science has found a temporary solution to this pandemic. We are slowly returning to a new normal. There is, however, no guarantee that we may not face another world challenge.

The important thing that we may well be missing here is how we are looking at these happenings. Are we looking at this period the way we should? Is all this part of a larger plan?

Are we simply reacting and scrambling to find a solution using logic and rationale? Or is there a truth that is open to us that we are failing to see? Maybe, just maybe there is a totally different way to look at this.

What is it that we are seeing happening around us? Reduction of vehicles on the road and air which has lessened air pollution. More animals, birds and insects are thriving with less human interference in the forests. Nature is recovering. People are spending less on frivolous wants. Family units are staying together and learning to live harmoniously.

Agreed, the earth is getting hotter, natural resources are being destroyed. War and strife continue to batter some countries. Natural disasters continue wrecking their havoc. The pandemic has not changed all that.

Yet, much has changed in terms of our lifestyle. However, there are some constants. The sun and moon are not going anywhere. The oceans are not going to dry up. For, the story of creation cannot end abruptly.

For the next chapter – The Age of the Thinking Man to begin, another foundation is being laid. It is not what we expected. It is not a happy transition. But then, man has brought it upon himself with the misuse of free choice.

Maybe we must learn many more lessons like the current one, before we can progress to a better stage. Looking at the world we have created now, we may be in for a long run of challenges. Because the lessons have not been learnt - yet.

And so, the cleansing process will continue. We may face more natural disasters, more diseases before Material Man finally realizes that he must change.

But will that change happen? Yes. For, no matter how much Material Man has messed up, God's plan is always good. Material Man will one day awaken.

Then, mankind will no longer blame Satan for the evils that exist in the world. He will understand that Satan is not an entity with horns and tail that he thought it to be. Man needs no help from Satan to create the evil that exists in the world. He has done it all by himself! All Satan or Maya did was obscure Man's divinity from himself.

Man, the microcosm of the macrocosm, has with his ability to create, created mayhem. What Satan could induce man to rape a week-old infant? What Satan can induce man to murder his fellowmen for just the 'joy' of it. What Satan can induce man to amass endless fortune that he cannot really enjoy?

For, the created man can only sleep on one bed at a time. He can only live under one roof at a time. He can eat only that which his body can handle at one time. Yet, there are those who live in homes that can easily accommodate 10 families, while others are homeless, with no food and shelter.

One man earns millions and has a fleet of cars, another trudges on foot trying to make a living. One man has dogs that are groomed, and fed better than another man, who is starving, covered in filth and lives on streets. Somewhere, Material Man lost his direction. And he has still not regained it.

Man has become so conscious of his body, that he has lost sight of his higher perceptions. We have unnecessary obsession for different types of diet. We have unnecessary need to clothe ourselves with expensive fragments of tattered clothes, and paint our nails, and wear different shoes for different occasions – all in the name of fashion.

The pandemic came as one of the lessons to bring man to his senses. This was a time when there is no opportunity for man to show off his wealth. People were not even able to visit each other. So, all money that man has spent on himself and his home, seemed wasted. He was unable to go to celebrate events; and all those expensive clothes and shoes stay in the closets.

While unrestricted misuse has created imbalance in the physical world, the same in social, economic, and political fields has created great imbalance in mankind. Much worse than all this is the greatest havoc that man has created.

In giving free reign to greed, lust and anger, man has lost complete sight of his divine heritage. So, is all lost? No, the creator's plan cannot be at fault. Even though man has unleashed mayhem in the created world, by ignoring the cosmic law, the creator will not withdraw his love from the created.

After repeated lessons, one day man will begin to understand that there is more to life than what he has hitherto perceived. As we are watching, slowly, one by one, people are finally trying to find the purpose of life. It is slow, but it will not stop.

Slowly habits will change, Material Man will start cherishing fresh grown food. He will stop feeding on life forms with gross matter, mainly bottom feeders like eels which according to some beliefs has very dirty 'prana' or energy.

Man will understand the importance of free flow of energy in his body. Physical exercise will start gaining more importance. Clothes will slowly become simpler and be made of natural fibers.

Owning more than one needs whether it is mansions, yacht's, fleet of cars, will one day soon seem insignificant, and in fact shameful. Material Man will understand that as long as there is still one more person living on the streets; one more person going without food, no one has the right to enjoy more than he needs.

Gone will be the need to erect statues when people are dying of hunger. Precious resources will be carefully preserved and cherished and shared. Things that are determinantal to nature will slowly stop being used. Scientists and inventors will start inventing more and more ecofriendly products. Mother Nature will finally start recovering.

Forced captivity of animals will be a thing of the past as man beings to respect all life forms. Wild animals will no longer be 'tamed' to perform unnatural acts for man's entertainment. Zoos will be more for rescuing and nurturing animals injured in the wild, than a place of cruel confinement in tiny areas.

In keeping with the preponderance of Material Man in disbelieving anything that is not proven by science, scientist will slowly start discovering more and more about the subtler planes.

Headlines like "scientists map one million new galaxies"; "an astronomer has searched the universe for a potential message from its creator"; "astronomers are mystified by these ghostly, unexplained circles seen in space", will become more and more common.

Material Man will find more and more 'new' ideas thrown at him like teletransportation and telepathy. Good times will come. Mankind will progress. But it may not be in our lifetime. It may take a hundreds of years for this transition to complete.

It may take many natural disasters and diseases to finally push man to the Age of the Thinking Man.

The Age of the Thinking Man

A time will come, much, much later when Material Man will finally evolve into Thinking Man. He will be the better version of the Material Man. Only because, he has finally learnt his lesson.

Seeing the world change in different ways will have shocked the Material Man into seeing the errors of his doings. As he loses people all around him and as he sees the world population start shrinking, man will come to his senses.

Gone will be the obsession to hoard material things. Man will understand that fashion or a fancy car is not going to give him happiness. Man will learn simple living. He will understand that this world is only a transient place.

He will understand that it is in giving that he will gain. Sharing will become more common. The imbalance and gap between the rich and poor will slowly start shrinking. He will know that this physical world is only transient. He is just journeying through this world until he can become one with the creator.

The seven lights will continue their work. Now, they will be more visible. For now, they know that Material Man is finally evolving into what the creator had always intended.

The Thinking Man will focus on changing himself. Drugs, alcohol, and other intoxicants will slowly make their way out of society. All these negative habit making activities that are detrimental to mankind will lose their allure.

Thinking Man will begin to see the unity in the teachings of all religions. He will draw the best from each one of them. From Christianity he will learn love and forgiveness, from Buddhism compassion.

Islam with its beautiful religious edicts on regular prayer, fasting and ban on drugs and alcohol will give its knowledge to others. Hinduism will continue to draw upon its vast store of knowledge of mysticism and yoga. Judaism will reinforce the concept of one God.

Taoism will help man understand the importance of 'Now' and what it means just to 'Be'. From the native tribes, Thinking Man will relearn that all life forms, including the one that he depends on for food must be respected. As science continues to make discoveries, even the atheist will know that positive change within himself is the most important factor of life.

The Age of the Thinking Man will see a gradual shift from body consciousness to soul consciousness. There will no longer be endless discussions on gender equality, feminism, or gender identification. For, man will finally begin to understand that within him is present both the masculine and feminine principles. And that the body is just a garment for the soul. That it is time to nurture the soul, without being too inordinately obsessed with the body.

He will slowly begin to learn to live right and eat right. And he will take care of his body, but once he has kept the body healthy and well, he will pay no more heed to it. He will thank the animals and plants he eats for giving him sustenance. In a way, he will have come a full circle from early Material Man who practiced this – thanking of the nature for its bounty.

The family system as we know will change gradually. The idea of growing up, getting a job, getting married, having children, and then growing old and dying, will not be the goal.

Conscious effort will be made to have good thoughts during the act of conception to bring souls that are better suited to a higher vibration of living. Man will understand the importance of the state of mind during the act of conception.

He will know that the thoughts of the man and woman during that time attract souls with similar propensities. He will know that children are an important part of the future of this world. They will be cherished and nourished not only in body, but in mind and soul.

Taking a step away from only the 'self', Thinking Man will want to set goals that will make a difference to him and the world around him. His focus will change from all the mundane aspects of life.

Scientists will start figuring out how mankind can exist in extreme temperatures. More methods of sustenance will come into being. Thinking Man will strive to preserve what is left of precious earth.

More and more men will seek to understand that which is beyond the five senses. They will seek out different spiritual paths. Focus will move from going to religious gatherings to worship, to quiet worship at homes. Every home will gradually become a spiritual center. Music will be more melodious and will no longer create discordant notes. Art will be sublime.

Education as we know today, which focuses on dry learning, will change. Efforts will be made to inculcate good habits and lofty ideals in eager minds. Education will be focused on all round development. Subjects that have no practical use in daily life, will slowly be discarded. Life skills, including high ideals, moral science and good behavior will be more important than getting high grades.

Reincarnating souls will be of a higher aptitude, crossing barriers of learning faster than it was possible for children born during the era of the Material Man. Those that never changed during the time of the Material Man will no longer be invited into the womb of a new mother. Their gross vibrations will no longer be able to tolerate the higher vibrations of the evolving human body. Hence, those souls with higher vibrations will start populating the earth. They will usher in the next beautiful phase of life – the time of The Universal Man.

The Universal Man

By now, the world will have seen so much change. A few thousand years will have passed, and evil acts of men will become exceedingly rare. Negative forces will try to surface here and there but there will simply be no room for them to grow.

The world will no longer have geographical and political barriers. Race and ethnicity will no longer be discussed, because mankind will have evolved to the time of the Universal Man. All will be equal. Love will no longer be confined to one's own 'blood'. For man will know that every created being is connected to the creator. In one sense, all are brothers and sisters.

He will know that those familiar to him were once connected to him in other births during his evolution. He will know that they were freely interplaying different roles in each birth. In one birth a father, in another a brother or a child in yet another.

He will know that the two extremes of love and hatred brought them all these souls back together over and over. He will learn that the only way to break ties that will keep them reincarnating to work out their ties, would be to expand his love. The tie will not break until he finally learns to love without attachment and has learnt to love those that he once hated.

Perhaps, someone will reflect that it was this that made a mother give unconditional love to her wayward child during the age of the Material Man. Or that is why a family may have siblings that simply cannot get along. They will understand that these are individuals who have been given a chance once again to work out their animosity and replace it with understanding. And that is why they are born in relationships where love is taken as granted in the social framework.

Religion will exist in the way it was meant to be. To provide a

69

framework and guide spiritual aspirants on the journey back to the creator. Universal Man will take the best that each religion has to offer and use that which he finds beneficial for his growth. He will no longer be curtailed by blind faith.

Even though, all men were created equal during the period of the Material Man, it will not be until the Age of The Thinking Man, that this truth will finally start sinking in. By the time of the Universal Man, this truth will be understood by every living man.

The knowledge of the seven lights will now be more accessible to all men, for man will finally be ready to receive them. The Universal Man will know that all those historical figures that he marveled at, where in fact avatars of these seven lights.

He will know that Christ, Krishna, Muhammed, Buddha, St. Francis of Assisi, St Theresa of Avila, Paramahansa Yogananda, Ramakrishna Paramahansa, Gandhi, Martin Luther King, were all avatars of the seven lights that descended into the physical plane to bring forgotten truths to the world.

Interestingly, of these, only Agastya will remain constant in his appearance. His name will be repeated through the different phases and he will appear in the same form. He will be the one continuous awareness through the entire process. Perhaps as a reminder of our divine heritage. Or we will perhaps know it was for a different reason before the end of this cycle of creation.

The earth will reach sublime heights of knowledge in all fields. Mankind will finally see what heaven is because it will be seen all around him. For, Universal Man will have created heaven on the earth plane by his ways.

By now, communication between created worlds will have become common. Aliens that the Material Man sought, will be the universal brothers of the Universal Man. The Thinking Man will finally know the mysteries of the world. He will know how to draw energy from the energy centers in the world. He will intuitively know that which seemed inexplicable to the Material Man from the remnants of the Era of Gods.

Before long, every created man will be a walking creator. So high will be his awareness of his self. It is then the need for creation to continue will become unnecessary. For man will understand that he is part of the creator. He can never be destroyed. That kernel, that soul that was part of the creator that was emitted during creation to become the entity called man, will once again merge, and become one with that great power – the omnipresent, the creator.

End of This Cycle of Creation

So will come the time for the end of this cycle of creation. After all the different transitions from ignorance, to learning, and finally the knowing, the created are ready to return to the creator. The work of the seven lights is done-for now. Their work done; they will return to the creator in an instant.

Meanwhile, the dissolution of this cycle of creation will start with the slow hum of the primordial sound reverberating all over the earth. All animals, birds, reptiles – nay, all life will come to a standstill, as they hear the great sound of the creator.

Slowly, with the spreading sound will come the effervescent light glowing all around. Great peace and joy will envelope the entire universe. As the glow becomes stronger and stronger and the sound of creation grows and grows, the world will vibrate at higher and higher speeds. The gross matter will vibrate and change to finer vibrations, the finer vibrations to the ethereal and finally – there will be nothing. Just a void.

And that is BEFORE creation starts all over again. And the countless who perished during the Era of the Material Man, without reaching the stage of The Universal Man, will now be ready to start their cycle all over again. Between now and then, my dear reader, is a long, long 'time', as we know it.

At this juncture I would like to add that while these chapters on creation, evolution of mankind and the future of mankind are all my imagination, great ones have revealed some specific truths connected with this.

The one I found to be true is the information presented in the book "The Holy Science" by Sri Sri Swami Yukteswar. He is my Guru

Yogananda's guru. Hence, my Paramaguru[39].

Based on his book, we can safely accept that in a matter of another eight thousand years, as Sri Sri Swami Yukteswar says, "mankind will comprehend God and the spirit beyond the human world". Until then, we will ascend step by step as more and more of the mysteries that were once hidden are revealed. The discoveries that are being made by quantum physics, astronomers and scientist are an indication of that ascent.

❦

---

[39] Paramaguru: A guru of one's teacher. Hence part of the lineage of gurus of that tradition.

OUR PATH FORWARD

What About Us?

If you have come this far in this journey with me, then you are with me in thinking that you do not want to do this all over again. How can we escape this eternal cycle?

The great news is that we have already begun that journey. Whether we know it or not, accept it or not, every human is on the journey back to the creator. For some, it may happen in this cycle, for others, in the future cycles to come. Eventually, it will happen.

For those of us who would rather do it now, the very fact that we are attracted to subjects like this has moved us up on the ladder of spiritual evolution.

Think about it, there are several layers of spiritual evolution that can be seen all around us. Lest we forget, we have passed through those stages ourselves. All of us. There is much to be learnt and experienced and fulfilled before we can finish this journey.

What are the different layers of spiritual evolution that we can see? Keeping in mind that none of them are higher or lower in any way, but merely steps that all must take, let us take a quick look.

There are some of us, that do not even believe in the existence of anything other than what we can perceive through our senses. And that is okay.

There are yet others, that are propelled by faith and ritual. These brothers and sisters, go through life without questioning their origin or their end. They go to religious places of worship diligently and perform rites and rituals without fail. They try to lead good lives.

Then there are those that have begun to seek. In that very seeking is the final phase of our journey, albeit a long one depending on our own progress.

They seek through books, like many of us do. They seek through the company of like-minded souls. They seek through the words and deeds of the seven lights, in whatever region or religion is dear to them.

Then come those that take deliberate steps and choose to follow a spiritual path to find that final liberation. Or, sometimes, even to understand a little more than that they perceive through their senses.

Among them are many who may have been diverted from their onward journey for some time. Enamored by the different powers or faculties that open up during spiritual practices, they may spend time enjoying these fruits, without making the effort to reach the destination. Such is the allure of the different faculties that one achieves in the spiritual path - clairvoyance, clairaudience, visions, experience of miracles, and finally, contact with God. Yet, most of them are resolutely on their way back to the creator.

Finding our Path

How does one do that? How do we find the path suitable to us? There are so many religions. There are so many paths. So many methods. Which is the correct one for us?

Well, for true seekers, as it is said in India, "when the disciple is ready, the master will come." He may come as Christ, or Krishna, or Mohammed, or a Yogananda. It does not matter in what form the guide comes to us.

And believe me, every one of us needs that guide. Whether we learnt to walk, talk, or swim, we needed someone to teach us. In the same way, we will have someone to show us our path and guide us through this final phase of our journey. There is no harm in exploring different methods and ideas to find a path. Once we find it, we will have no doubts that it is the correct one for us.

However, just as it is important to adhere to one method of practice to achieve perfection in anything, so also in spirituality. After all, focus and one pointedness is the key to everything. Hence, once we find our path and have no doubts about it, it is important that we walk on it until we reach our destination.

Meditation, no matter what we call it is the key. Some may call it yoga; others mindfulness; still others Zen or transcendental meditation. Or it could be a meditation class with its own unique name at the place of worship. The name does not matter. All are based on the same idea, and they are all methods to reach the same goal.

While we are on this journey of exploration of our paths, is there anything else we can do to prepare ourselves?

We Are the Lights

We can prepare ourselves every day, every moment. Spiritual life is not divorced from our everyday life. We can be the little lights that are quietly shining in different corners of the world.

The great lights are lighting spiritual lamps in individuals all over the world. They are among us. They are like us. We too are the lights. It is simply a matter of letting our light shine through. The light is in all of us, just waiting to be discovered.

How do we know a human lamp that has been 'lit'? By the effect, such people have on all those around them. These are the individuals that leave us refreshed every time we meet them or spend time with them. These are individuals whose smiles light up the spark of joy in your own heart. These are the individuals who seem to add more to our life in one way or the other.

It is that woman who rescues and nurtures wounded animals; it is that man who does not hesitate to jump into the ocean to rescue a stranger; it is the child that gives its candy to the homeless person. Or is simply that person who is patient and kind and genuinely cares about our day.

These little lights may not even know that they are the lights of the quiet spiritual revolution that is taking place. They may not be aware that the light of God is shining through their beautiful hearts. These are the lights that are making the world a better place, creating islands of peace in this chaotic world.

What makes them different from the rest? They are constantly trying to be better. To be kinder, to be nicer, to be forgiving, and to reserve no judgement in their hearts. They fail, sometimes. But they never give up.

Where do we start in letting that light shine through?

Reflection. When we are lost in some thought, let us stop for a moment and identify where that thought came from. It will be interesting to see how one small thing has triggered a whole chain of thoughts!

So, that is where we begin. We begin by watching our thoughts. Not in a fanatical way. We do not want to become obsessed with it. Let us become more aware of them. And then when we realize that what we see, hear, touch or smell triggers thoughts, let us take care that we give room only for good thoughts to grow. Which means, we become gatekeepers of our senses. If we look at 'advertisement', it is based on this idea — of how to create a 'need' or 'want' in someone for a product. Hence, those delicious pictures of food that tempt us.

As gatekeepers, we begin by watching what we expose ourselves to. Good thoughts lead to positive actions. So, we now know that thought and action are interconnected. So, the best way to develop good habits is to focus on those things that help us cultivate good habits.

Books, people, movies, resources on the web, there are umpteen number of avenues for us to develop better thoughts, and through them better actions.

The next step is to understand whatever we do affects others around us. If we are upset or angry, not only do those around us see it, but they can also feel it. So, let us always try to be positive.

I have personally found that when negative thoughts invade, it is best to either spend time reading, listening to uplifting music, or even watching some inspirational movies.

Books especially carry the vibrations of the author. A book written by a great thinker, can influence us no matter if thousands of years have passed since it was written. We do not have to look further than our own scriptures. Everything that we need to know is already there in them.

We can also try to ensure that our actions do not hurt others. This means we stop ourselves when we want to retort in anger or want to be sarcastic. It is not easy. But with patience and repeated attempts, we can change.

Or very simply, we can choose to emulate any one of the characteristics of the great lights. Even that will change us for the better. And in changing ourselves, we will change our surroundings. And that light of love, compassion and kindness will spread. It is this that the world needs right now.

Meanwhile, our own paths will be revealed to us and we will have prepared the soil for the seed of spirituality to sprout and grow. And before long, we will reach our destination. We will return to the creator who made us all.

Let us also do another sacred duty if we are fortunate to be parents. Let us bring our children into the light. Today, the world needs people with values more than anything else.

Accomplishing this is amazingly easy. In reading inspirational stories to our children, encouraging them to cultivate in an interest in the arts, setting an example of goodness, we can do much more for the world than by focusing on their grades and careers. Those will follow naturally if we but instill good values in our children. Because the future of our world is in our children.

Let us light that lamp in each one of these beautiful angels. For, indeed they are, the lights that will change the world!

And as Sage Agastya says,

"The initial flame of supreme knowledge belongs to the creator. It flows through the great lights, seen and unseen. You are all part of this wonderful cosmic intention. Once the lamp is lit, the flame can light indefinite number of other lamps".

MEDITATION - THE BEGINNING

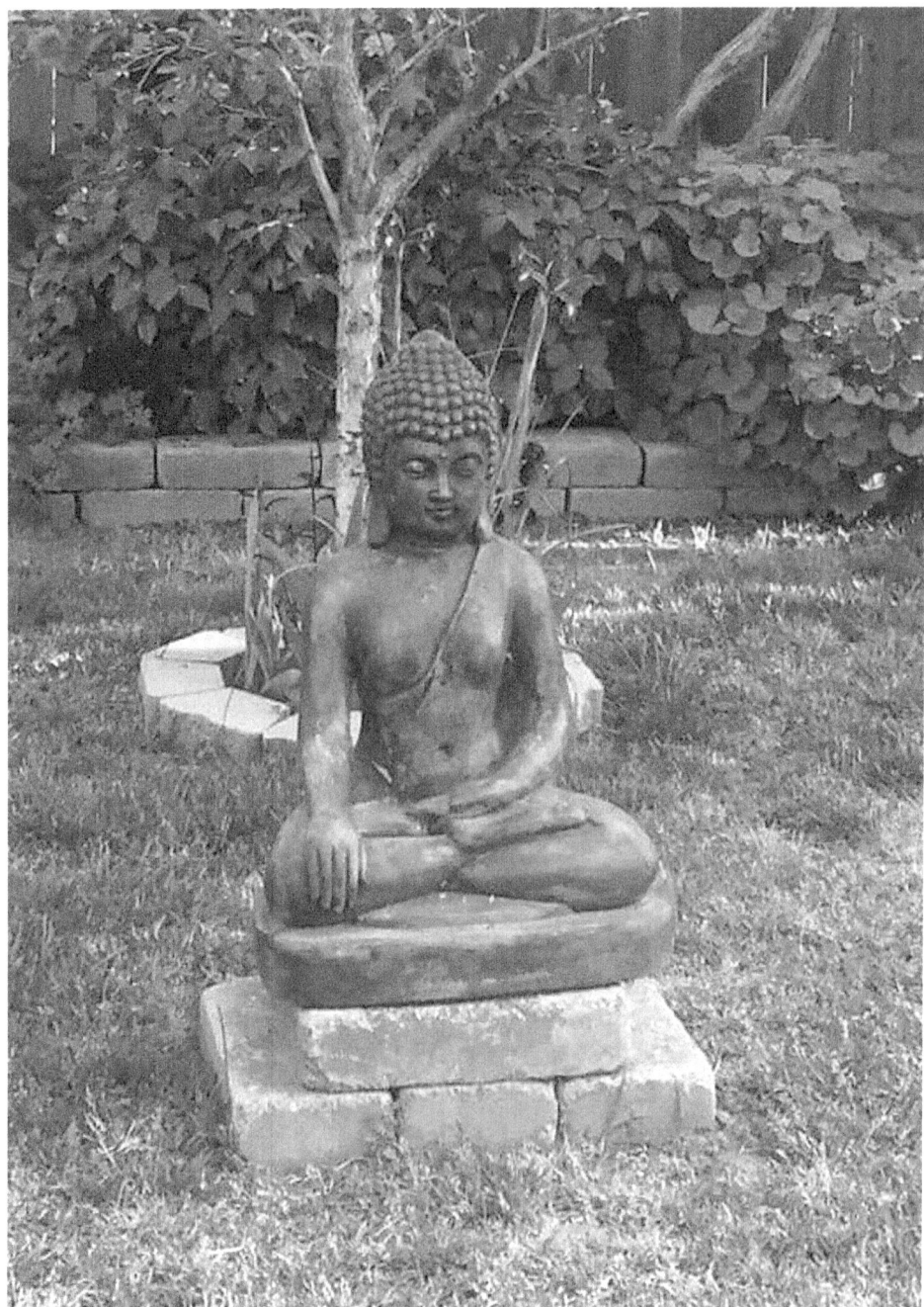

How Do We Begin?

For earnest seekers, meditation is the path to self-realization. And it is a means to return to reach the ultimate goal of liberation. Here are some basic guidelines for beginning meditation at home that are universal in nature.

1.Location: Every place has its own vibration. Hence it is important to identify one spot in the house that is not normally used for day to day activities. It could be small quiet corner, or a room dedicated to meditation and prayer. An altar can be set up if space is available. And until a path is found, it is best to keep either a lamp, or one item, that evokes devotion. It is important not to clutter the altar with too many things since these cause visual distractions.

2. Time: Habits are formed by repeated action. A good habit to form is dedicating the same time every day for meditation and prayer. Just as our habits trigger the time to eat, we can train ourselves to have a specific time devoted to meditation and prayer. Again, it is important not to become too fanatical about it. If the desire to meditate or prayer comes during other times of the day, then it is simply a matter of going to that spot and sitting down.

3.Posture: A comfortable posture helps keep the mind focused on meditation. Any posture whether it is sitting on a chair or sitting cross legged on a mat works. However, the most important thing to note is that the spine must be always straight. Energy is concentrated at the base of the spine and we want that energy to travel up to the crown of the head during meditation. The methods for doing this are thought by different schools of meditation. Chin must be parallel to the ground and eyes closed and focused on the middle of the forehead.

4. Breathing: This is a key in mediation. Until a specific type of meditation practice is learnt from a master, it is best to watch the breathe as it goes in and out.

5. External factors: In the modern age, it is especially important to

85

ensure that the external world does not intrude in your practice. Turn off anything that creates noise, turn off cell phones. The world will still be there after meditation, and phone calls can be returned after meditation.

6. Aids to devotion: A lamp, a flower, a candle or even a picture of Christ, Krishna or any other God may be placed on the altar to evoke devotion. Light music especially flute, or a chanting of Aum or even a recording of waves are a great aid to meditation for beginners.

7. Length of meditation: The length of meditation is never the factor, the depth matters. It is best to start with ten minutes dedicated to meditation and slowly increase it over time.

8. Thoughts: Regarding the proverbial problem of thoughts. Let them come, but do not follow them. Bring your mind gently back to the object of your focus.

It is best not to expect wondrous visions or experiences during the initial stages of meditation. For some just sitting quietly may seem like a waste of time. Yet, it is in stillness that we progress

More important than all this, is bringing attention back to God through the day just as the thought of a lover always remains in the back of one's mind.

The path meant for us will be eventually come. Meanwhile, it is best to explore different groups of meditation to seek the path that appeals the most. When the right one comes along, there will be no doubt in your mind.

❀

Exploring Meditation Paths

Meditation sessions and retreats offered by places of worship are a great place to start the practice of meditation. Churches offer retreats and meditation classes. So do other places of worship.

Devotional gatherings also help increase the fervor of the soul in seeking liberation.

If neither is possible, there are many ways to start on the path. Reading about the life and teachings of great saints like Saint Francis of Assisi, Mother Teresa; reading the works of poet-philosophers like Rumi, Khaleel Gibran, Meera, Kabir; studying our own scriptures like the Bible, Koran, Torah, Bhagavad Gita – the resources are endless.

There are countless mindfulness and yoga centers for beginners that offer meditation classes around the world. These serve to lay a foundation as one waits for the 'call' from true realized masters.

At their best, these meditation centers help manage day-to-day stress levels. However, it is important to remember that teachers that are not self-realized cannot lead one on the path to liberation.

Some links to a few universal meditation groups established by great masters is given on the next page. They are by no means exclusive and are laid out in alphabetical order. There are many others around the world that one may explore.

As true seekers, it is best to always learn from an established certified teacher belonging to well-known and tested organizations. Many of them offer free online classes and meditation sessions.

Some Meditation Groups

Amma: A spiritual organization founded under Mata Amrithanandamayi, who has hugged over 30 million people in the world. Her teachings are also universal and does not require anyone to change their religion to follow her teachings. Her Amrithapuri Ashram is located in Parayakadavu village in Kerala in India. She teaches the Integrated Amrita Meditation Technique for spiritual advancement.

amma.org |

Brahama Kumaris: Brahama Kumaris is a worldwide spiritual movement that is based on the principles of Raja Yoga. It is open to all faiths. Founded by Dada Lekhraj Kripalani, it has its headquarters at Mount Abu in Rajasthan, India. They have centers around the world. The largest spiritual organization led by women, the organization helps individual transformation from materialism to spiritualism.

Brahma Kumaris - Home

International Zen Association: Practiced worldwide in Zen temples and monasteries based on teachings of the Buddha. The practice is focused on concentration, and introspection. These teachings were brought to China by Bodhidharma and to Japan by Dogen.

History of Zen Buddhism | International Zen Association (zen-azi.org)

Ramakrishna Mission: Based on the teachings of the realized master Sri Ramakrishna, this organization offers universal worship methods. This order was established by Swami Vivekananda. His opening sentence at the World Parliament of Religion in 1893 drew standing ovation for several minutes. Sri Ramakrishna who is known as the prophet of harmony of religions, was a Hindu mystic saint in the 19th century in India.

Ramakrishna Order Centers Worldwide

Self-Realization Fellowship: Organization founded by Paramahansa Yogananda in 1920 to impart scientific methods of mediation and principles of living. He taught Kriya yoga, the direct path to God realization that was revived by Mahavatar Babaji and then given to the world by Larhiri Mahasaya. Yogananda's book "The Autobiography of a Yogi" has drawn countless followers to the path including Steve Jobs and George Harrison. Self-Realization Fellowship which has its headquarters in Mount Washington in Los Angeles, California has centers worldwide.

Home | Self-Realization Fellowship (yogananda.org)

Sahaj Marg: A yogic system of meditation by Sri Ram Chandraji of Fategargh in India. As its name indicates, it is a natural path of meditation. It is universal without religious and cultural connotations. His successor was Sri Ram Chandraji of Shahajapur fondly known as Babuji. Sahaj Marg centers are found worldwide.

https://www.sahajmarg.org/

Sri Aurobindo Ashram: Founded by Sri Aurobindo in 1926, the Aurobindo ashram in Pondicherry in India teaches Integral yoga which transforms a man's nature while liberating his consciousness. His most famous disciple Mirra Alfassa known popularly as 'The Mother', continued his work.

https://www.sriaurobindoashram.org/

Sri Ramanashram: Teaches the direct path of practice of self-enquiry. His teachings are disseminated at the ashram located at the base of the Arunachala hill which is considered the spiritual heart of the world. There are centers worldwide where devotional gatherings are held.

https://www.sriramanamaharshi.org/

Transcendental Meditation: Founded by Maharishi Mahesh Yogi, Transcendental Meditation is a simple, natural, effortless technique of meditation. It is promoted as an effortless method which is personalized on an individual basis.

Transcendental Meditation® Technique – Official Website (tm.org)

Twin Heart Meditation: A method of meditation developed by Master Choa Kok Sui, world master of Pranic healing. It is promoted for its simplicity that gets great results. It helps cleanse the aura of individuals to help experience higher level of awareness.

twin-hearts-meditation-benefits (worldpranichealing.com)

Vipassana Meditation: Is based on the teachings of Buddha. The word Vipassana itself means insight which enables one to discern. It was popularized in Burma in the 1950s and is promoted as helping reach direct knowledge.

Vipassana Meditation (dhamma.org)

Glossary of Terms

Aum: the primordial sound. It is said to be the sound of creation itself. It is the Amen of Christianity and Amin of Islam.

Himalaya: A snow covered mountain in northern India which stretches over Pakistan, Afghanistan, China, Bhutan, and Nepal. The world's tallest peak in the world is located here: Mt. Everest.

Hindustani music: A classical style of Indian music of Northern India, famed for its arrangement of tunes. These are basic tunes called Ragas, and have different features that evoke emotions, and are said to have control over the elements when sung with intense devotion.

Mantras: Sacred chants that are repeated with the right inflection to produce tangible results.

Pranic healing: A system of healing that uses life energy (prana as it is known in India) to cleanse and remove diseased energy from the human body. This ancient system of healing was rediscovered by Grandmaster Choa Kok Sui in the 70's. MCKS Founder | Pranic Healing

Vedas: Ancient Hindu scriptures that are said to be directly revealed to sages of India. There are four major Vedas. Rig Veda is the oldest extant text on the origin of the universe and hymns to Gods. The others are Yajur which contains details of different rituals and hymns; Atharva procedures for everyday life; and Sama Veda which consists of hymns in a melodious form.

Yoga: A system that helps unite the individual consciousness with soul consciousness. It is a Sanskrit word that has now been accepted in English in its original form. The word originates in India where the science of Yoga teaches that there are four main types of yoga. Raja Yoga, Karma Yoga, Gnana Yoga and Bhakti Yoga. Raja Yoga or the path of the king, is considered the foremost and entails practicing different methods of meditation, breathing and postures. Karma Yoga is yoga through service. Gnana yoga is practice of acquiring knowledge and Bhakti yoga is reaching God through devotion.

Further Reading

The Holy Science: Sri Swami Sri Sri Yukteswar Giri

This phenomenal book provides actual understanding of the cycle of the universe. This God given knowledge has been shared by Swami Sri Yukteswar in a language that is comprehendible to all. The good news is that according to Yukteswar in this book, we are now in the ascending cycle of creation. The exact years when changes take place are also indicated in this book.

The Autobiography of a Yogi: Paramahansa Yogananda

This timeless classic published in over 50 languages, has touched millions in the world. IT giant Steve Jobs, and George Harrison of the Beatles were influenced by it. Many truths that are incomprehensible to the modern mind, are given in vivid details. It is truly a life changing book.

Books on spirituality by Parmahansa Yogananda

Man's Eternal Quest

The Second Coming of Christ

God Talks with Arjuna

Journey to Self-Realization

Divine Romance

On Pranic Healing by Grandmaster Cho Kok Sui

The Ancient Science and Art of Pranic Healing

Miracles Through Pranic Healing

Pranic Crystal Healing

On Theosophy

By C.W. Leadbetter

The Use and Power of Thought

The Chakras

By H.P. Blavatsky

The Seven Planes from the Theosophy

The Secret Doctrine

By Different Authors

Einstein And the Poet: William Hermanns

Hands of Light: Barbara Ann Brennan

Illusions: Richard Bach

Magic & Mystery in Tibet: Alexandra David-Neel

Nothing by Chance: Richard Bach

Raja Yoga: Swami Vivekananda

The Prophet: Kahleel Gibran

The Wandering Taoist: Deng Ming Dao

What Men Live By: Leo Tolstoy

Acknowledgement

No life exists in a bubble. The family we are born in; the environment we live in; the people we meet are some important factors that shape our lives. I was blessed to be born to spiritual parents. I was fortunate to be exposed to both the deep spiritual Indian culture and the vibrant independent spirit of America.

What I am today and what I write about is because of all the people in my life. I would like to thank the many individuals who helped a new immigrant facing many personal challenges assimilate in the United States.

When I left India, I thought I was leaving my home and family. Yet, when I came here, I realized that everywhere was home and all were my family.

My thanks to the Dr. Bala Iyer and his family for welcoming strangers into their home without a second thought. My cousins Vani David, Madhu Arun, and Resh Wallaja for their timely advice. Sadhana Mazumdar who heard about me and helped without any hesitation as did the D. Narasimhan family.

Stepping out into the wider society, I found family all around me. Dr. Sudarshan Kapoor and Veena Kapoor were beacons of light, guiding me to one of most memorable relationships in this life with Grace Longeneker. She was in her early 80s when I met her. She was American and I was a new immigrant with a teenage daughter. I spent nearly a year with her. She was my mother, friend, mentor, and guide.

Parishioners of the St. Paul Newman Center welcomed a stranger that I was, with open arms. Monsignor Perry Kavookjian who was then our Parish priest was open to my idea that I wanted to know God as a Christian. Director of Ministries, John Prandini; Sr. Rosemary DeGracia now Oblate Director at Annunciation Monastery; Connie

Mollo; my sponsor late Frank Clark; my spiritual brother David Fredrick; Larry Langford; Charles Arokiasamy and his mother late Mary Arokiasamy were some parishioners who played a special part in my life.

The staff of Fresno County, chiefly Rosa Amaro, John Manivong, Julie Thao, Rebecca Renovato and Mona Tarango made me feel I belong.

Donna Rimmel Mormon, my first friend in this country and Kiran Johal, both have remained great friends. They welcomed a stranger as a friend and held me close to their heart.

I would be amiss if I do not make a special mention of Maryann Villegas whose keen eye in editing and invaluable suggestions has given the important finishing touches to this book. My heartfelt thanks to Lillian Fillpot, PsyD, Health Educator for taking time to read my manuscript and write the foreword to this book. My daughter Sahana Ashok Nayak for tweaking some of my writing to make it more appealing.

A special thanks to Basawaraj Musavalgi, Retired Dean, Chamarajendra Academy of Visual Arts (CAVA), Mysore, India for illustrations on page 16 and 46. He very graciously gave me permission to use his artworks. Both have been altered from their original dimensions to suit the needs of this book. Artwork on page 16 has the original title: Floating Object, medium: Photography. Artwork on page 46: Original title: Tsunami, medium: Computer graphics.

Also my heartfelt thanks to my spiritual brother Harish Bheemaiah for the photograph on page 76.

Last but not the least, the Lopez family for accepting me wholeheartedly into their fold. And as always, my husband Arthur, daughter Sahana and stepson Aaron for the joy they bring me.

About the Author

Anuradha Gajaraj-Lopez lives in Clovis, California. She was a journalist in India before she emigrated to the United States. She was born into a spiritual family and nurtured with ideals of Indian spirituality.

She graduated from Mysore University in South India and holds a postgraduate degree in Journalism and Mass Communication. She is a disciple of Paramahansa Yogananda, the great Yogi who is known for his book "Autobiography of a Yogi".

Some of her poems were published in the Theosophical Society – American section quarterly magazines, before she started publishing books of her poetry, prose, and fiction.

Books by The Author

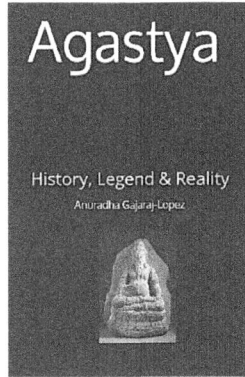

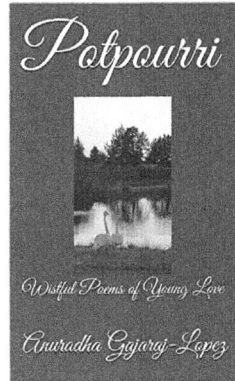

DIVINE BLOSSOMS
Call of the inner voice:
A collection of inspired poetry
Anuradha Gajaraj-Lopez

Agastya
History, Legend & Reality
Anuradha Gajaraj-Lopez

BHAJANS
English Transliterations
ANURADHA GAJARAJ-LOPEZ

Potpourri
Wistful Poems of Young Love
Anuradha Gajaraj-Lopez

COMING SOON

Beads of Meditation: Reflections on life

Agastya's Devotee: Firsthand Chronicles of An Extraordinary Life

Made in the USA
Middletown, DE
02 July 2021